OTHER BOOKS
BY THE SAME AUTHOR

Coplas
Tales from Count Lucanor
My House Is Your House
I Am Maria

AWAY IS SO FAR

AWAY
IS SO FAR

Toby Talbot

Illustrated by

Dominique Michele Strandquest

Four Winds Press ~ New York

Library of Congress Cataloging in Publication Data

Talbot, Toby.
  Away is so far.

  SUMMARY: After his mother dies, a young boy and
his father leave their Spanish village and set out to
wander to forget their sorrows.
  [1. Fathers and sons—Fiction. 2. Spain—
Fiction] I. Strandquest, Dominique, illus.
II. Title.
PZ7.T148Aw   [Fic]   73–88072

Published by Four Winds Press
A Division of Scholastic Magazines, Inc. New York, N.Y.
Text copyright © 1974 by Toby Talbot
Illustrations copyright © 1974 by Dominique Strandquest
Library of Congress Catalogue Card Number: 73–88072

AWAY IS SO FAR

S etting the tin pitcher of milk on the ground, Pedro paused in front of his house. This morning, as every morning, he was returning with milk fetched from a village farmer. But today his mother had not roused him. For his mother was dead. Gone. A whole month it was since her funeral, and almost a year that she'd been ill. Now he and his father were alone. And sadness nested in this house of theirs.

Pedro pushed open the door and placed the milk, still frothy and warm from the cow, on the kitchen table. The house was still. His father must be sleeping yet. Ordinarily an early riser, since Mama's death he slept late. He doesn't want to start the day without her, thought Pedro.

Pedro's eyes swung to the picture of his mother and father hanging on the wall. His father was smiling that once familiar smile, now vanished, and his mother looked so young and pretty. Pedro hungered for her and longed to feel her touch. It was hard to believe that he would never see her again. Sometimes he had the feeling that she had simply gone down to the village and would return shortly. Yet here in the house, thinking, handling objects she had once used, he felt her presence. He preferred being in the house to playing outdoors.

Kindling a fire in the *nafre*, their little charcoal stove, Pedro poured the milk into the pot and set it to boil, the way his mother had always done. He could almost hear her praise his skill. *"Bueno, Pedro, bueno."*

He reached now for the watering can alongside the sink and set it under the tap. The water gushed inside and Pedro carried it out to the patio to water his mother's pots of basil and carnations, and last of all, the geraniums. He plucked the faded blooms and yellowed leaves, and then poured the water over the parched soil which sucked it up thirstily. It was going to be hot today and it was best to water early, before the mid-day sun heated the water and scorched the roots. Pedro sniffed his fingers; he loved the pungent geranium smell that clung to them. It made him a bit heady, like incense in church.

Back in the kitchen he placed two bowls on the table for breakfast, one for himself and one for his father. As the milk bubbled Pedro gazed into its whiteness and remembered how she used to melt chocolate in the hot milk and give him a biscuit to dunk. Suddenly a voice broke the stillness.

"Pedro, is that you?"

"*Sí, Papa*, it's me."

A gaunt man with dark circles shadowing his eyes entered from the other room. He wore a band of mourning on his arm.

"Good morning, Papa," said Pedro. The ritual words sounded silly as he looked at his father's pale face, eyes sunken from sleeplessness. What he really wanted to say was, "Oh, Papa, how I miss Mama. When I'm in bed at night, I feel so alone. What's going to happen to us?"

But the words didn't come. For in the last month Pedro often stopped himself from saying what was on the tip of his tongue. How different from before when he could say anything to his father. Mama used to say that Papa was so gentle and knowing that he could hear the flowers grow. But now he seemed cut off from everyone. It was as if an invisible sign were posted on his face forbidding certain things from being said.

His guitar, once bursting with song, stood

voiceless in the corner—its mouth yawning, its strings mute.

His father sat down heavily. "Good morning, Pedrito."

This day, Pedro could foresee, would be like all the others since his mother died. After breakfast, his father would pace restlessly about the house. Then he'd drift out to the fields and mechanically begin to plow. But suddenly he might halt in his tracks, lean on the plow and simply stare off into space. From a distance Pedro had seen him that way the other day, standing still as a scarecrow.

He poured his father's milk. "Can I get you some biscuits, Papa?"

"No, Pedro, I have no hunger."

Pedro blew on his milk and gingerly took a sip. "I'll pick up a bread on my way home from school, like yesterday."

His father shook his head. "Today you're not going to school," he said in a flat voice.

Pedro set down his bowl of milk. "How come? What do you mean?"

"Pedro, we must go away. Here in this house, in this village, my sorrow is too great."

Pedro, stunned, stared at his father. How could he say that? Surely he couldn't mean it. This was where they belonged, it was where Pedro was born . . . and where his mother had died.

"But, Papa, we can't leave. This is Mama's house. It's all we have of her."

His father shook his head. "No, Pedro, we have our memories of her. And those are inside us."

"But her grave is here in the village!" The words came blurting out on their own.

His father's face went chalky white. "I know, I know . . . But we won't be gone forever. We'll be back."

"It'll be too late though. The house needs a fresh coat of whitewash, and the artichokes have to be planted, and I'm in the middle of school . . ."

His father rose and cleared their dishes from the table. "Everything can wait, Pedro. Things have already slipped in the last year, as you know. They'll only slip a little more."

Pedro knew that his father was referring to that day almost a year ago when Mama's illness began. The doctor in the hospital, after examining Mama, had shook his head, which meant her illness could not be cured. Other doctors were consulted. And then Mama came home. But even in her illness she acted as if she were going to live a long time. Only towards the end had she stayed in bed . . . Pedro watched his father now as he methodically began to rinse their dishes. The water rattled loudly against the tin sink.

Pedro remembered during his mother's last days overhearing her tell his father, "I want your lives, after the first nine days of mourning, to go on normally." And Pedro recalled another time, long before she fell ill, when she had expressed her disapproval of the custom of prolonged mourning common among many families.

"She wouldn't want us to go away," Pedro protested. "She'd want things to be kept the same."

"She would understand. It's hard to explain. You are only eleven years old. But without Mama I can't go on doing the usual things in the usual way. I haven't the heart for it. You are the only one I care about. And you will be with me."

There was a long silence. "What good will it do to go away?" Pedro asked, almost in a whisper.

"Every beam in this house, every corner, reminds me of her." His father's voice broke with emotion. "Away from home, the pain will be less sharp. Maybe I can forget a little . . ." He paused and brushed his thumb across his cheek, a habit of his when he was upset. "I'll take my guitar, and play it here and there to earn our bread. We'll manage."

Pedro couldn't imagine his father playing the guitar for money. But as his father spoke, Pedro recalled other instances when he had evoked the wandering life. For in his youth he had been a wandering minstrel, a *tocador*. And he had loved to reminisce about those roaming, carefree days. Particularly when times were bad.

Once when the summer drought was very severe, and all the artichokes withered on the stalk, his father in great disgust had ranted against the life of a farmer and bemoaned the day he had exchanged a *tocador*'s free existence for it. But then Pedro's mother had teased him and called him a vagabond and a gypsy. And she told a story about a certain witch she knew who flew about on misty nights on her spinning reel, and who had taught her an authentic spell to bring on rain. Whereupon Pedro's mother had closed her eyes and in a singsong voice recited a funny charm which she assured them, with eyes twinkling, would bring on the rain. Papa muttered against women's *brujerías*, or witchcraft, but wound up laughing anyhow at Mama's spooky tone and expression. And before long he was strumming away at his guitar, singing gay tunes with funny verses which he invented.

Mama had a knack for making people feel good. Pedro tried to think of what she would say now. "Troubles get solved where you are," he said, "not by running away."

"My head says *yes* to you, Pedro, but my heart says *run*. That's how it must be, come what may."

Pedro listened helplessly. If only he could cry out that he didn't want to leave, *he didn't want to leave!* His mother no longer lived in her body, but her love still dwelt here. Nobody was ever gone completely . . . But as Pedro looked at his father's determined face, all his answers faded away. He knew that this time there was no swaying the *tocador*. He had made up his mind.

Pedro walked over to his mother's sewing basket and nervously picked up a piece of string. It was the string he and she always used when they played cat's cradle. Pedro unraveled the string and without raising his eyes asked, "Where shall we go?"

"I don't know."

So vague was this reply that Pedro bit his lip as he always did when worried. His mother, rather than scold him about the habit, had always tried to distract him. His father, however, didn't seem to even notice the little drop of blood that Pedro could taste on his lip as he bit harder.

Papa was now completely preoccupied in getting ready to leave. Placing a blue-checked cloth on the bed he began to pack: shaving brush, soap, two sweaters, his and Pedro's, and from the pantry he took a parcel of food which, Pedro suddenly realized, must have been prepared the night before. How long had he been planning this move? His father now put on his heavy boots, tied up the knapsack, shouldered his guitar and handed Pedro their water flask to carry. It was all so fast. Pedro stood there numb, his arms dangling.

And then his father went and closed the shutters of the house. With the sun blocked out the room was thrust into darkness.

From the threshold Pedro took a last glance at his mother's things: her sewing basket, her apron, the heavy fringed shawl draped on her chair. As he hovered on the threshold, images of her flitted through his mind like the pages of a photograph album: Mama walking, or rather swaying, to the village well with the double-nozzled clay *cántaro* on her hip, Mama scrubbing the floor clean and then laying a fresh straw mat on it, Mama stretching the wash on a fig tree or on the pebbles in the patio to bleach it white in the sun, Mama on the rush chair darning, patching, reinforcing Papa's work clothes so that they would last forever, or, on that same chair, peeling potatoes, sorting lentils, firing fish for lunch.

"Come, Pedro, come!" His father's hoarse voice jolted him from his reverie.

Pedro faltered. How long would they be gone? Would they ever come back? In his confusion he dropped the water flask he was carrying. Hastily he stooped to retrieve it, and in rising, his shoulder bumped against a little table that stood by the door. The blue-and-white vase on top of it, one his mother had cherished, smashed to the ground. Pedro winced and held his breath. An instant later he fell to his knees and clumsily began picking up the pieces.

His father stared at the scattered shards of pottery and gave a low groan. "Leave it, leave it, let's go!" In his agitation, his nails were digging into Pedro's shoulder as he prodded him into the street. And then, as though startled by his own force, before Pedro could utter a cry or complaint, he abruptly let go. "Did I hurt you?

I'm sorry. I didn't mean to." The words, remorseful, came in fits and starts. Pedro shook his head and refrained from rubbing the spot.

Once outside, his father reached for a key that hung hidden on a nail of the window ledge. Then he locked the door. Nobody in their village ever locked their doors, and the harsh, unfamiliar grating of the key in the rusty lock rasped in Pedro's ears. At that moment it seemed as if the house too had died. It was empty now, without people, bustle, noise, cooking smells, life. Pedro felt as if he were betraying it.

His father turned to him. "I know you want to stay, but . . . I can't," he said sorrowfully, and led Pedro off with him.

They began to climb the steep zigzagged streets of the village. Pedro felt the ascending sun warmly on his back. Its benign early morning rays tinted the laundry-white houses creamy yellow. It was going to be a balmy day. There was no sadness in this clear sky. How could his mother be dead under this beautiful sky?

As they walked Pedro realized that his father was leading them toward the road that ran high above and parallel to the Mediterranean Sea. The winding village extended its long streets as if to detain them from plunging into unknown space. Where were they going? Would they ever see these streets again?

They came to the house where the old dressmaker lived with her rabbits, chickens and a pig called Ana. Last Easter the dressmaker had sewn a blue dress for Pedro's mother. . . . In front of a house further on, Antonia, the baker's daughter, was singing and sprinkling down the dust. She waved to Pedro and his father, but did not interrupt her song. Pedro had known her all his life. She was especially happy these days, for she was about to be married. In other times, Pedro's father would have played his guitar and sung at her wedding. But now they would miss it.

As Pedro and his father neared the schoolhouse Pedro heard someone hailing him from behind.

"Pedrito, wait for me."

It was his good friend, Marco. He came running, breathless.

"Whew! Am I glad to see somebody else is late for school," gasped Marco, shifting his load of books. "Why don't we slip in together? The teacher will scold us less."

Pedro glanced at his father uneasily, and slowed down. "Uh . . . I'm not going to school today."

"How come?" asked Marco, and then, suddenly recalling the death in the family, "oh, I understand . . . But say, I have to hurry. I'm going to get in trouble. It's the second time this week I'm late. See you later."

Pedro's father had walked on ahead while Pedro lagged behind in conversation with Marco. Hurrying now to catch up with him, Pedro heard through the open school window the chanting of the youngest children in the school. *Three plus three is six, three plus four is seven, three plus* . . . What would Marco say if he knew that Pedro was leaving, maybe forever?

Now they passed the gypsies' caves and then the last village wall, all crumbled and knobbly with stonecrop. And then they reached the road that followed the sea. The bamboo fringing it rustled as Pedro and his father tramped along, and some oxen in a nearby meadow, still silver with dew, bellowed hello or, Pedro wondered, was it goodbye? A fisherman's wife, the one they called "La Gorda," the "Fat One," was rocking her baby to sleep outside her house. Pedro hadn't seen her since the day of the funeral, when she wore a black mantilla on her head. Her husband had been one of the pallbearers in the funeral procession. Now she called out, "*Vaya con Dios*," go with God, the traditional village greeting.

"*Vaya con Dios*," Pedro called back, but his father said not a word. Pedro glanced sidelong at him and colored. Nobody ever ignored that common everyday politeness. It violated custom,

and was tantamount to an insult. Without thinking, Pedro turned and waved goodbye to "La
Gorda."

And as they struck out on the road Pedro
thought he heard her sigh and softly utter,
"*Ay, pobrecito!*"

They walked on and on along the dusty road, following the coastline going north. Below on their right the jagged rocks plunged down to the sand where some fishing smacks were moored. Here and there Pedro could see an exhausted fisherman, sprawled under his hull among the nets, sleeping after his night's labors. And beyond that stretched a blue-green sheet of glass, the Mediterranean, serene, unaware of death, rippling out towards the infinite horizon.

As the gulls glided and dipped over the water, Pedro wished that he could become a gull. He would fly straight back to his village and go to his mother's grave. They had left without going there, without even taking a snapshot of her. He turned to look back at the village.

The village in the distance looked like a picture in a storybook, and the bell tower of the church that lorded over the red-tiled roofs was a mere squiggle in the sky. Seeing his father pause too, Pedro turned to say this to him, but as he looked at his father's face, he seemed so buried in thoughts of his own that Pedro kept silent.

What was he thinking, Pedro wondered? His distant expression gave not a clue. Was he making a plan for their voyage or would they simply be strays like those poor scrawny dogs that sometimes roved into the village, scrounging for food and then suddenly vanishing?

The noon sun, directly overhead, blazed down and Pedro's feet in their canvas, rope-soled *alpargatas* were starting to burn. Just as he thought he could trudge no more, his father slowed down near a brook.

"Do you want to rest?" he asked.

"Yes, Papa."

Out of the knapsack his father drew a cold potato omelette, bread and sausage. Silently he took his penknife from his pocket, cut two slabs of bread, two chunks of spicy *chorizo* and divided the *tortilla*. With a gentle look in his eyes he handed Pedro the heel of the bread, Pedro's favorite part.

"*Gracias, Papa,*" said Pedro, touched by his father's show of caring. He bit into the crusty end and then, out of habit, found himself uttering one of his mother's favorite proverbs, "The best sauce is hunger."

His father looked up and, to Pedro's surprise, responded automatically with the companion proverb, "And the best wine is water." Pedro nodded and handed his father the canteen.

The familiar phrases seemed to stir his father from his isolation. He gazed at Pedro. "Most boys are *hijos del pueblo*, loyal sons of their village, as they say. But to me you are truly your mother's son. You resemble her and at times even talk like her. I am glad."

"She always thought I looked like *you*," said Pedro, comforted by the words.

His father leaned back against a tree and ate quietly. Now that they were under way, he seemed somewhat relieved. He raised the canteen to his mouth and then passed it to Pedro.

Pedro drank and then, encouraged by his father's mood, turned to him, "Papa, can I ask you something?"

"Hmmm?"

Pedro hesitated a moment. "Will we be away long?"

"Ah, Pedro boy, we have a far way to go. Our first stop will be Málaga, and then the open road."

"Do you know your way?"

"Don't worry, Pedro, I'll take care of you."

"I know, Papa." His face became hot and he picked up a stick and began to jab the earth.

After a few moments his father said, "It's a good thing you don't catch cold easily."

And Pedro, falling into a more conversational tone, went on gratefully, "No, the last cold I had was in November of last year when our house flooded."

"Ah, yes, during the rainy season."

"Remember, after the flood stopped how we had to sweep the water out with brooms? Everything was so damp we all caught colds. Me, Mama, even you."

"Yes, I remember . . ."

"The mud outside didn't dry for weeks. And our feet were always caked with mud, even though you stretched planks all around the house."

Pedro's father looked down at his own feet, and then at Pedro's. "And now, Pedro, they're covered with the dust of the road. You should have shoes for the journey. But we need money for that . . ."

His voice trailed off and he lapsed into silence. Then lying down heavily on the ground, he assumed his typical siesta position: propped on his left side, the right arm tossed over his body. In a few minutes he dropped off to sleep.

Pedro sighed and he, too, stretched out under a tree near the stream. The earth smelled of flowers and loamy depths. Pedro smelled it and felt like crying. He picked up a stick again and began drawing a picture. He tried to draw his mother. But in no way did it come out looking like her. Under the picture he wrote, *Mama*.

Suddenly a small emerald-green lizard crawled over to the spot where he was drawing. Pedro placed his hand in front of the lizard and the little creature crept up on it. The roughness of its dry scaly skin sent shivers up and down Pedro's back and made the hair on his arms stand on end the way it did when his teacher squeaked the chalk against the blackboard. Yet Pedro wanted to hold on to the lizard, and each time it reached the end of his hand and pre-

pared to crawl off, Pedro placed his other hand
in front of it. Left hand, right hand, left hand,
right hand . . . He kept the lizard on its endless road. It was a wanderer, like him and his
father. At last Pedro allowed it to topple over,
and when he did so it landed upside down. He
watched it struggle to right itself and then he
helped it. The lizard scooted away. "Lucky
little fellow, you are saved. Hurry home,"
Pedro whispered.

Suddenly the drowsy afternoon was nudged
awake by the choking and wheezing of a motorcycle which pulled up alongside the brook. The
driver dismounted and, acknowledging Pedro
with a friendly nod, went over to the brook.
He crouched down to the water, drank, filled
his wineskin and then proceeded to pour some
water into a nozzle in the back of his motorcycle.

"Even animals on wheels get thirsty," he
winked to Pedro.

Pedro nodded.

In a few moments the motorcycle was off

again like a balking bull. As it raced down the
road Pedro wished he were on it. It looked so
exciting, and the man seemed so lighthearted,
not like . . . Pedro cut off his disloyal
thought, before he could conclude it with "not
like his father." He felt a twinge of guilt.

At that moment his father stood up, having
been awakened by the noise of the motorcycle,
but not stirring until it had gone. He collected
their things.

"Come, my son, I want to reach Málaga before the sun sets."

Pedro took the knapsack and the canteen.
"Yes, Papa."

Fortified by their meal and the rest, Pedro
began wondering what Málaga looked like.
None of his friends had ever been there. As he
and his father resumed their journey, somehow
the walking seemed easier. The trick, he decided, was to keep looking ahead to find little
destinations. How many steps would it take to
reach the clump of blossoming almond trees on

the hill ahead, or the giant *chumbo* cactus that dominated the crossroads, or a woman in the distance carrying a bunch of thyme, lavender, and rosemary down from the hills for kindling? Walking thus became a guessing game. And the final goal was Málaga.

Every now and then from behind them a rickety bus marked *Málaga* came coughing down the road, loaded on top with valises, baskets of fruit, and coops of squawking chickens. In a while they approached a sugar factory with three smokestacks ejecting black curlicues onto a bright blue sky. And then they came to a factory designated by a sign with a picture of grapes and the words: *Uvas de Málaga.* Crates upon crates of Málaga wine were stacked in front of it.

"Well, this is it, Pedro," announced his father. "The first stop on our long journey."

The houses that now lined the road, un-like the little whitewashed houses of Pedro's village, were connected three-story dwellings, looped together by clotheslines.

The road bent to the right and then abruptly, as though a fan had been twirled open, the harbor of Málaga sprung before them, dotted with boats on the seaside and fringed with palms on landside.

"Look, Pedro, look over there." His father pointed. "See the Cathedral of Málaga?" In the melting light the great single tower spiring in the distance seemed to be floating toward them.

With renewed energy they started walking along the boulevard that rimmed the harbor. Sleek, jingling horse-drawn carriages clattered over the cobblestones. The gleaming spokes of the wheels flickered under the lacework of the lofty trees, and the horses, their heads thrown back, were more elegant than any Pedro had ever seen. People sat on stone benches leisurely watching the passersby. Pedro wouldn't have minded sitting down, too. His steps slackened.

"Come, Pedro. Don't dawdle." His father took his elbow and guided him toward a busy thoroughfare. There, spotting a lottery-vendor, he raised his beret. "*Buenas tardes, señor.*"

"*Muy buenas,*" the man replied. "Would you like a five *céntimo* ticket?"

"Another day. But, tell me, *señor*, where is the principal café."

"Oh, you must want the Café Central on Calle Larios, corner of Serrano." The man pointed to their left where a broad avenue, the main street, ribboned through the city.

They turned into Calle Larios, lined with old stone buildings, the upper floors scrolled with iron balconies, the lower with shops. In one window mannequins, their faces rouged by twilight, were smiling out at Pedro. The church-bells began to chime six times. It was the hour of the *paseo*, and the streets undulated with people out for their evening stroll. As Pedro passed nursemaids in starched white pinafores wheeling babies in strollers and couples sauntering by arm-in-arm, it reminded him so much of the walks he and his parents used to take.

Noticing Pedro's reflective expression, Pedro's father paused as they passed a glass-fronted casino where some old men seated on cane chairs were playing dominoes. It was a game familiar to them both.

"Well, Pedro, what do you think of Málaga?" he finally asked.

"It's so beautiful, and big."

"To a village boy it's big. To a man from Madrid it might seem quite small . . ."

Pedro waited for him to continue, but he did not. Pedro was growing accustomed to his father's fragments of conversation and silences. They alternated like the ebb and flow of the sea. At one moment his words would surface and Pedro felt close to him, but a moment later his father again withdrew into the depths of his sadness.

Suddenly Pedro felt lost and frightened. He reached for his father's hand. His father pressed it. "Don't be afraid, Pedro," he said quietly.

The Café Central was an imposing establishment. A green-and-yellow striped awning graced its exterior, and little marble-topped tables were spaced underneath.

His father took a deep breath. "Let's go inside."

Pedro followed uncertainly. The new intensity in his father's voice startled him. Inside, men in dark suits, starched shirts and silk ties sat at the tables. When they wanted service, they clapped their hands and a waiter in a spotless white coat hurried over and brought them cognac or coffee. Lovely women in flowered dresses were sipping sherry and nibbling from little plates of almonds, olives and shrimp. Around a bar people were laughing and chatting.

Pedro's father unstrapped his guitar. Pedro watched him tune up as he had watched him countless times. He placed his fingers on the frets, turned the screws on the neck of the guitar and plucked the strings, cocking his head intently as he sought the true notes. And then the guitar was struck.

Pedro listened to the piercing tones. It was like an eruption that had been muffled too long. The guitar wailed like the wind over the sea. It made Pedro tremble.

He stared at his father, who was standing with legs planted firmly, head thrown back. From the guitar he coaxed forth notes clear and

pure. The guitar was speaking for him, it was his other voice, uttering all the feelings so painful to express.

This was not the familiar man Pedro saw day in and day out patiently plowing and irrigating their fields, who strolled arm in arm with a friend in their village square, or who allowed Pedro a sip of his wine at their local café. This was Juan, the *tocador*, the public figure, the performer. A man with a new identity, a look of authority. And he was not playing the happy folk songs he had played for Pedro's mother, but sad ones, laments.

> *Cada vez que considero*
> *Que me tengo de morir . . .*
> *Tiendo la capa en el suelo*
> *Y me harto de dormir.*

> Each time I consider
> That I must die . . .
> I stretch my cape on the ground
> And sleep and sleep.

Pedro recognized the tune of the ancient
copla at once, as did the audience, even though
the words weren't sung. Pedro studied his father
as the notes of the guitar rose in swift runs, de-
scended in sudden catches and died away in a
long note that mingled with the sounds of the
café and the city.

Some men sipping wine called out, *"Olé,
tocador!"* Pedro looked proudly at his father.
He was an artist. An artist with the power to
move men, to animate the wood and strings of
his guitar, to make them vibrate and sing under
his skilled fingers.

When the song was over, the men at the
tables signaled to Pedro. *"Ven acá, muchacho."*

Pedro hesitated, and looked toward his
father. His father nodded. Shyly Pedro walked
over to them. They held out some shiny coppers,
but he felt ashamed, like a beggar, and turned
away.

"No, Pedro," his father spoke firmly. "I am
a *tocador*. And a *tocador* is paid for his music,

for his art. Take it. We have earned the money."

"*Toma, toma, muchacho*," a man urged him gently.

Pedro took off his beret and collected the coins. As he was finishing, the owner's wife approached.

"Would you play me a tune, amigo?" she asked the *tocador*. "A *malagueño?*"

"Certainly, *señora*," Pedro's father bowed. He moved toward a vacant chair and rested one foot on it.

The guitar broke into the classic folk air of Málaga. Everyone listened attentively. When he was through, a string of *olés* burst upon the café, and the owner's wife, a woman with kind eyes, gave Pedro a bill for twenty *pesetas* and a sandwich of bread and chocolate.

The woman turned again to the *tocador*. "And now will you sing?"

Pedro's father frowned. "I don't sing. I'm a musician, not an entertainer."

Pedro was shocked by his father's brusque

denial. He remembered the days when his father's deep voice had echoed over the fields as he worked, as he walked with Pedro on the hills, as he mended a broken chair, or plow.

His father had an unlimited stock of songs and could go on singing them for days without repeating himself. He knew many songs of only four lines which took a long time to sing, for they were performed with endless improvisations and intonations. Would he ever sing again? And thinking of that beautiful voice, now silenced, Pedro's throat knotted and could not swallow the bread and chocolate offered him by the café owner's wife. Then recalling his mother's songs, tears welled up in his eyes but never fell.

When they left the café Pedro held the guitar while his father sorted and counted the money they had collected. A pleased look was on his face, and Pedro ventured to ask, "Why were you so angry when the woman asked you to sing?"

His father clucked his tongue impatiently. "I'm in no mood for singing. Let's drop the subject." Pedro, feeling rebuffed, dropped his head. It was a mistake, he realized, to try to talk about certain things with his father.

"Never mind, Pedro. Look, we've collected seventy pesetas. Counting the one hundred we started out with, that makes one hundred and seventy pesetas. Now one hundred and seventy pesetas can buy a laying chicken, a hutch of rabbits, a month's supply of charcoal, or . . . a pair of shoes."

Pedro glanced at him, puzzled.

"If we hurry, Pedro, we can catch the stores before they close."

He hustled Pedro down Calle Larios, and before he knew it Pedro found himself seated in a shoe store, and having his foot measured by a salesman who seemed to regard the dusty foot with disdain. Pedro suddenly felt terribly ashamed of those dusty feet of his and felt like sitting on them. Indeed the salesman made them buy a pair of socks before he would even allow Pedro to try on the shoes. And then he tried to convince them to buy a pair of shiny black patent leather pumps with pointed toes which, he explained, were perfect for Sunday wear.

"We want a sturdy pair of walking shoes made of bull-hide," Pedro's father insisted. And moments later that's what Pedro walked out in.

"How do they feel?" asked his father.

Pedro grinned. "Like somebody else's feet in somebody else's shoes." And then he couldn't resist adding, at the risk of spoiling this light moment, "If only Mama could see me in my first pair of leather shoes."

To his surprise his father nodded, but corrected him. "As a matter of fact these are not your first pair of leather shoes. *She* was the one who bought you those, when you were eight months old and starting to walk. White calfskin they were and about the size of my middle finger. You howled the whole time the shoe salesman was fitting you."

Pedro laughed. "I sort of felt the same way today too." He rocked back and forth on the balls of his feet, drawing little squeaks from the new leather. "I guess these shoes are a little tougher though than the white calfskins."

His father nodded. "You'll have plenty of opportunity to break them in," he said.

The blackness of night was now falling. Pedro looked around at the closed shops and cafés, at the majestic ghostly façades.

"Where shall we sleep?" he asked.

"Out in the open," said his father. "There is no pillow as soft as fatigue." And strapping the guitar to his shoulder he put his arm around Pedro's shoulder as they took the road out of the city.

"You are a good *tocador*'s companion," he remarked, picking up a knobby walking stick and handing it to Pedro.

"You are a good *tocador*," Pedro lightly returned the compliment, trying his best all the while not to stumble in his new shoes or trip with his walking stick. The stick was like a clumsy third leg. His father tousled his head, and in the dim moonlight Pedro thought he saw a smile soften his features, but the smile, if it was there, was gone quickly. And that veiled, unseeing look returned.

Soon they reached the outskirts of the city. Halting under a grove of trees his father looked around, "This is a good place to sleep."

Following his father's example, Pedro removed his jacket, stretched out on the ground and tucked the jacket under his head like a pillow. He gazed up at the sky. It was seeded with stars. Like little oil lamps, they were. And the slender horn of the moon tilted its light earthward.

Through his half-shut eyes the branches overhead formed a vague tracery. How unlike the shapes and shadows of his own room at home. Ah, how he missed those familiar cracks on his ceiling. He knew them as well as the lines on the palm of his hand; they seemed to outline

a horse's head. His mother had thought so too. The branches overhead rustled lightly. Pedro pressed himself tight against the ground.

As he lay there an owl hooted, a frog croaked, and a distant waterwheel in some field was creaking. Soon Pedro could hear his father breathing regularly, heavily. How Pedro used to love to fall asleep hearing his parents' low voices from the other room. But those days belonged to the past, to the happy days.

Pedro looked at his sleeping father. He wondered if his father dreamed about Mama. Though references to her were rare, Pedro knew that his father was thinking about her. He could tell. And yet his father reserved most of those thoughts to himself. It was as if he didn't want to share his sorrow—not even with Pedro.

But in April Pedro would be twelve. And when he reached twelve, Pedro had been promised a goat. He used to plan how he would take it down to the stream under the mountain where the grass was soft and the field was big and wide, and how he would sell the milk to the neighbors to make some money. But undoubtedly his father had forgotten his promise.

Pedro turned on his stomach and eased his toes deeper into his shoes. He'd forgotten to take them off. Drowsily he sat up, untied them and set them alongside him. As he lay in the darkness, the silhouette of his new shoes loomed large. In their upright position, they seemed ready to resume their journey. How far, mused Pedro, would those shoes go? Would they get all tattered and scruffy before he had a chance to show them off to his friends at school? Or maybe they would get so worn, they'd have to be replaced by a second pair, a larger size, and then by a third. How many nights would follow this first night away from home, how many miles?

And as Pedro gazed at his wayfaring shoes, his eyes blurred and the problem of distances dissolved. Softly the blanket of night unfolded upon him and he yielded to sleep.

The weeks went by. Pedro and his father walked every morning, stopping in some village in late afternoon to play at a café and earn money for food. Sometimes they would buy grapes or oranges, or fresh sardines which they cooked over a fire. But more often than not it was the nomad's diet: bread and cheese and smoked ham. They washed in the streams, and there Pedro's father shaved. If a stream were large enough to lie down in they would stretch out on the smooth washed stones of the bottom and let the cold rippling water play on them. When it was very hot they would take a siesta

under some trees or at times in a cave. The
wandering life had its joys.

But there were times when Pedro longed to
stay still. Once as they were leaving a little village halfway up the coast of Spain they saw
some men setting up stalls for a town fair.
Colored lamps hung from the trees and a Ferris
wheel was already in motion. A woman was
stoking a fire under a great iron cauldron and
the appetizing smell of frying fritters drifted
in the air.

Off to one side Pedro saw some gypsies cor-
raling a drove of horses and donkeys, probably
for a horse fair. When they were through they
clustered around one particular animal and ar-
gued hotly about how to teach it the tricks be-
fitting a gypsy donkey.

A few steps away two little boys began rolling on the ground, their fists flying. The trousers
of one were slit from top to bottom, leaving his
grazed shinbones exposed. The other, on top of

him, wore a red bandana on his head and nothing else except a man's vest. Pedro paused and smiled as one of the gypsies interrupted his argument, dashed over, and separated the boys. A young woman in a dotted and flounced red dancing dress appeared, gave the boys a few whacks, and led them off.

The whole scene looked so familiar and appealing to Pedro. The fair no doubt would last several days and there would be flamenco dancing and maybe fireworks. He turned to his father. "Papa, let's stay here for a while."

His father shook his head.

There was a silence. Pedro forced himself to speak. "Must we *always* be moving? Can't we ever stay in one place for more than a day?" He could hear the impatience in his own voice.

"No, Pedro." His father spoke slowly and deliberately. "We have no roots. And the high road is better than the inns. We must keep going and I must play my music."

On the road one day a peasant driving a mule-

drawn wagon loaded with melons passed alongside them. The mule had bright red pompoms
bobbing on its forehead to keep the flies away
and brilliant bands of color around its rump.
The driver was as weathered and wrinkled as a
leather wineskin.

"*Arre burro*," the man shouted to his mule,
waving at the same time to Pedro and his father.
Just then, from the opposite direction, a flock of
black pigs came charging down the road, a
young shepherd behind them, struggling to get
them out of the wagon's way. The mule pan-
icked at the onslaught of the grunting creatures
who were now bumping against the sides of the
wagon. With a jolt the animal veered to one
side into a ditch, the wagon overturned and the
melons began rolling helter-skelter on the
ground. The poor driver tore his hair and began
cursing his mule, the pigs, and his bad fortune.

"The world is full of hidden dangers, and
misfortune is my lot," he moaned.

"Don't worry," Pedro's father consoled him.

"My son and I will help you to gather the melons."

All three fell on their knees and finally had the wagon filled again, and the mule calmed.

"*Gracias, gracias,*" said the peasant, and invited Pedro's father to drink from his *bota*, the small wineskin he fetched from the wagon seat. Pedro's father tilted his head back and a fine stream of red wine trickled into his mouth.

The driver then rummaged among the pile of melons in the wagon and chose one. Thoughtfully squeezing the stem end to make sure it was ripe, he drew a penknife from his belt and cut a thick wedge from the rough green surface.

He watched anxiously as Pedro's teeth sank into the pale golden flesh. "Is it sweet?" he asked.

Juice oozed from the luscious melon onto Pedro's face. "Perfect," he smilingly assured the driver.

Then turning to Pedro's father, the man inquired, "Tell me, where are you bound for?"

Pedro's father handed back the wineskin with a nod of thanks. "Nowhere in particular. How about you?"

"France."

"Where's France?" Pedro asked the man, wiping his dripping chin with his handkerchief.

The man's arm swept northward. "Across the mountains and over the Spanish border. Can I give you a ride in that direction?"

"Why not? *Es igual*, it's all the same," shrugged Pedro's father. "The farther I go the better. A *tocador* has no home."

Pedro's heart sank. He couldn't believe what he had heard. France, that mysterious place, would swallow them up. His father didn't care where they went. If the man had said "China," they would have joined him too. His father, obviously, had no intention of returning soon, if ever.

"It's been a good harvest this year," the man went on cheerfully. "I'll get a fat sum for my melons in France. And I'll use the money to buy a young ox to help me plow my land."

Pedro listened enviously as the man recited his plan. Their land back home, unlike the man's, lay fallow, with no one to tend the little fig trees and pomegranates that his mother had planted.

But before Pedro knew it, they had all climbed into the wagon, his father in the seat alongside the driver, and he in back with the melons.

"*Arre burro*," cried the driver, clacking his tongue. The wagon was off with a jerk, and soon Pedro felt the wheels throbbing under him. Every once in a while a melon rolled off the heap and landed on his lap.

"Ah, I am just another ripe, juicy melon," he thought, and despite himself, found himself laughing and welcoming the unexpected ride.

They bumped along the road, passing villages that were blinding white in the sun, gnarled women who looked as ancient as Spain, windmills lazily slicing the hot air. Here and there a dog barked and came running after them. And then late in the day they noticed a charred cloud smudging the sky. It grew and grew until all the light blue turned dark blue and then black.

The peasant scratched his head and looked worried. "*Caramba*, there's a storm coming up. We'll have to take shelter at an inn. Luckily I know a *posada* nearby."

Upon their arrival he drove his cart into the stable. Pedro helped him unharness the mule and dole out some hay to it. Then they entered the inn. A fire was sizzling in the fireplace and from the ceiling rafters hung bacons, sausages and hams. The innkeeper, a lusty fellow with black whiskers, and smelling of garlic, red wine, and onions, brought some stew and wine to their table near the fire. Pedro gladly stretched his legs after the cramped wagon ride, and as he ate the hot food a flush of well-being settled upon him. After dinner, he leaned lazily on his elbows and watched the smoke rise from the fire, lingering and staining the rafters. His mother, he remembered, used to throw orange peels into their fire to make it shine as bright as Sunday! The men began to roll cigarettes and to talk over the table. It felt good to be in company. Things seemed normal and relaxed.

As the innkeeper filled them in on local gossip Pedro's father drew out his guitar and quietly started to play.

"*Estupendo, hombre,*" shouted the peasant. "You have magic in that instrument. Paris is the place for you. Parisians love Spanish music."

"That's what I'll do. Go to Paris." Pedro's father took a long puff on his cigarette and watched the smoke unfurl. "I've toiled with my hands for years, and what do I have? Nothing. *Nada, nada, nada . . .*"

Pedro bolted up at the toneless words. His chest tightened, and it was hard to catch his breath. Nothing? Not even him—Pedro?

"Don't talk like that in front of the boy,"

said the peasant. "Come now, let's have a song."

Pedro clamped his eyes shut. The rain sounded louder, and the voices more distant. "Oh, Mama," he thought to himself, "the rain just keeps coming down, and when it rains I want to be with you more than ever. Things are so terrible now. If you only knew . . . Here we are in a strange inn far away from home and Papa's words are so terrible. He thinks I'm nothing . . . And his music is so sad, sadder than you ever heard. Mama, I feel so alone."

Slumping into his chair, Pedro could picture vividly his mother's face, so close, so understanding. He sat quietly, and after a few minutes felt somewhat calmed. And suddenly his father's words the morning of their departure came to his mind. "You are the only one I care about. And you will be with me."

With his mother's face still before him, and in a half-sleep now, he whispered to himself, "It's not so, it's not possible that it's all nothing."

Early the next morning they harnessed the wagon and started out again on the road to France. When they reached the French side of the border the peasant drove them to the station and waited until they boarded the train for Paris. Pedro peered out the window and waved goodbye to him.

"*Hasta luego,*" their new friend called out. But, wondered Pedro, would they ever really see each other again?

As the train rumbled out of the station Pedro looked around at his fellow passengers, who were noisily settling themselves and their baggage. Most of them were boys, older than he.

They wore sturdy walking shoes and were unloading from their backs cumbersome packages bulging with saucepans, frying pans, folding tents and assorted camping equipment. The boys were boisterous and gay and spoke rapidly in a language Pedro could not understand, but assumed was French. It seemed like ages to him since he'd been with other boys. As he looked at them he felt suddenly shy. They seemed so self-assured. Pedro turned away so as not to attract attention and gazed out the window.

The train sped through russet valleys sprinkled with sparse vegetation, past rushing streams and then into a new fertile terrain where stone fences curbed grazing cattle, neatly tended vineyards, and cultivated hills. The cows looked fatter than those in Spain, and every inch of ground, up to the very railroad ties seemed thriftly utilized.

Every once in a while, Pedro poked his father and pointed out a scene. His father, however, was engrossed in changing a broken string on

his guitar, and answered indifferently, "*Sí, sí,*" or "*Hmm* . . ." Pedro glanced sidelong at the boys. How lucky they were to have company.

His mother had been such good company. They had spent so much time together, particcularly in her last year as her usual busy activity dwindled and she had to spend more time resting. They played cards or checkers in the patio, and on good days, when she was feeling stronger, she'd tell him stories about her childhood, and the scary witch tales passed on to her by her grandmother. At times when she was very tired, she'd lean back on her pillow and Pedro read the newspaper to her. It was hard toward the end to match that wan, frail mother with his former, rosy mother. And yet when she died it came as a shock. Oh, how he missed her . . .

The train, Pedro noticed, was gradually filling as it halted at villages to take on passengers, mostly peasants accompanied by goats and turkeys and lugging baskets of apricots, cherries, and cheeses. Pedro felt comfortable in their presence, even though they did not speak Spanish. At lunch time in true peasant tradition they offered him and his father bread and sausage and cheese.

For eleven hours the train rushed on. Forms and scenes lunged toward Pedro and were shoved aside by the advancing train. The abandoned images receded so quickly that he had no time to store them as landmarks in his memory. And yet, he thought, these were the places separating him from his home. What a trip this would have been if his mother were with them. The new sights would have excited her. She would have made it an adventure for Pedro.

In a fitful sleep Pedro heard the conductor chanting the names of unknown towns entered and departed: Toulouse, Monturaban, Quercy, Limoges, Chaterous, Orléans and then . . . Paris.

Eleven hours by train had brought him and his father from the border of Spain to Paris. On burro, eleven hours would be the distance from his own village to a remote mountain *pueblo* where they used to go to buy wool. And on foot, eleven hours was the normal span of a day at home. A day's comings and goings were like a circle, which began in the house, touched school, the fields, the market, and closed once again in the house. How far away that all seemed now.

The train began emptying out at the last stop. Pedro rose from his seat, his legs as wobbly as if he had indeed been riding a burro for eleven hours. He and his father followed the other passengers into a noisy and bustling railway station. Nobody in the jostling crowd appeared to be listening to the loudspeaker which was calling out train departures and arrivals in that same strange tongue, French.

"How will anyone understand us here?" Pedro asked his father as they elbowed their way toward the exit.

"Music is the language of God. We will be understood."

Pedro sighed. He felt hungry and dirty, and tired of traveling. If he could only settle into a hot sudsy bath and loll there for hours and hours, and come out only to eat a big *paella* of chicken and rice, like they used to have on Sundays. He looped his arm through his father's and allowed himself to be led.

Suddenly a woman wearing high heels stepped on his foot, uttered an apologetic *pardon*, and promptly vanished upon her high clicking heels into the crowd.

"Ow!" squealed Pedro and bent over to massage his injured toe. He gazed ruefully at the dusty battered shoe, not at all new anymore. "I guess that meant 'pardon me.'"

"You've just learned your first French word, the hard way." For a moment his father's eyes twinkled. One word was a small beginning, Pedro thought.

As they passed through the revolving doors and found themselves in the open air, he breathed more easily. To his surprise the street near the station seemed quite commonplace. He had expected Paris to be spectacular, exotic. They began to walk and at the corner Pedro noticed a pastry shop. Fragrant, mouth-watering smells of hot fresh dough, cinnamon, and butter wafted forth. His belly growled. Suddenly his father turned to him. "Would you like something?"

"*Sí, Papa*," Pedro nodded sheepishly, ashamed somehow of his uncontrollable growls. It seemed so unmanly.

Inside, the proprietress eyed them suspiciously. Pedro felt out-of-place in his baggy clothes. No boy that he'd seen here wore *alpargatas* or a sash around his waist. His father too looked shabby in his corduroys.

Pedro's father pointed matter-of-factly to several pastries in the showcase and paid the woman for them. Outside they found a nearby bench and sat down. Pedro started with the strawberry tart, quickly polished off the cream puff and then munched on some almond macaroons. France, he decided as he licked some powdered sugar from the corners of his mouth, might not be so bad.

While eating they watched the passing scene. Automobiles scooted by honking their horns, and in the middle of the street, mounted on a little platform, a policeman with white-gloved hands directed the traffic.

"Look, Pedro," said his father, nudging him. "There's a café down that block. Let's go over. Maybe I can play."

They crossed the street and when they came to the café Pedro's father went over to a waiter and pointed to his guitar as if to ask permission to play. The waiter looked at them askance, shook his head emphatically, and signaled for them to move on. Pedro's father shrugged.

"Don't worry, Pedro. We'll find another café. Paris is big."

They began wandering about in the strange city. As they walked Pedro's first impressions altered. Paris was indeed grand. Its buildings were majestic, its roofs festooned with lavish details. Ornate moldings, graceful balustrades, carved cornices and scrollwork ridged the sky. Fashionable people, all apparently in a great hurry, brushed past them as if there were no time in their lives for music.

In a while they found themselves on a wide boulevard, the Champs-Elysées, according to a street sign. Pedro had never before seen such a long street, an endless succession of cinemas, hotels, automobile displays, banks, airline offices, shops filled with gowns and furs. They passed café terraces too, but they were so imposing that he and his father dared not stop.

On and on they walked through a grove of chestnut trees and into a large square. Pedro's eyes swept over every structure in it and with awe: a columned palace, a temple with archways and pillars and even a stone obelisk. A red, white and blue flag fluttered over the spectacle.

His father set down his guitar a moment and surveyed the square. "We're a long way from our village, eh Pedro?"

"*Sí, Papa,*" Pedro answered. He couldn't help thinking of how much there would be to tell his friends one day. He could almost hear himself, and his tone was boastful.

"Look over there." His father pointed to a bridge ahead of them. They started across.

Midway they stopped and gazed upstream and downstream. Every mile or so a glittering bridge spanned the water.

"This must be the Seine River," said his

father. "It divides the city in two, the left and the right banks. Come, let's go to the other side. Maybe we'll find a café there to play in."

On the opposite bank they strolled along a quay lined with booksellers' stalls. After a while they paused again and leaned over the stone balustrade to look into the waters of the Seine. Tugboats were floating by, and launches filled with sight-seers. On the embankment below, Pedro saw solitary men fishing, a young man and woman picnicking, and a tramp peacefully sleeping. On the opposite bank a beautiful cathedral with stained glass windows rose amid the pinkish-gold haze of evening. Pedro, succumbing to the quiet scene, relaxed in the warm drift of air.

A jolt at his side, however, suddenly made him turn. His father, he noticed, was staring oddly into the water and at the people meandering on the banks of the river. He seemed to be looking particularly at a boy flying a kite. The boy was accompanied by his mother. The woman

in many ways resembled Mama, Pedro thought
—her height, her dark hair coiled loosely at her
neck, the way she walked. As his father watched
the pair, his face darkened and then he winced.
"Papa, what is it?" asked Pedro, frightened by
his expression.

"Nothing." He seized Pedro's hand.

"Your hands are so cold, Papa."

"I'm all right. Let's move on." Pedro quietly
followed him, feeling more and more con-
cerned.

They began wending their way through
cobbled sidestreets with their shop windows
spilling over with old maps, buttons, and
mounted butterflies. How unlike his village,
thought Pedro, where shop windows displayed
only necessities. Several men passed on bicycles
with long breads tied to the backs—that looked
much more familiar.

They came now to a square with a fountain
in the middle and four cafés around it. His
father halted.

"Let's stand right in the center by the fountain, Pedro, and I'll play. Who can chase us? The fountain belongs to no one."

"That's right, the fountain belongs to everyone," put in Pedro in a deliberately assertive tone, hoping to boost his father's spirits.

Poising his guitar, the *tocador* surveyed the clientele of the four cafés with a knowing professional glance. Even to Pedro they seemed well-to-do. He moved off a few steps to give his father center stage. The *tocador* struck up a traditional folk dance, a *bolero*.

The Frenchmen sat nonchalantly at their tables eating and sipping coffee. Their conversation continued as his father played, and their cups and saucers tinkled loudly. Not one person appeared to be paying the slightest attention to the music.

Pedro was shocked and furious. What an insult! Where was their respect? How could they ignore a master guitarist? In Spain this would never happen. Pedro worriedly looked at his father. His shoulders sloped down at sharp angles, and his head—the hair now grown long, the beard stubbly—hung to one side. Though frowning, he continued to play. Still the audience prattled away. They seemed so smug, so deaf.

Uneasily, Pedro scanned his father's haggard face again. His bloodshot eyes blazed. Two spots of fire were imprinted on his cheeks. Pedro had never seen him look so feverish and defiant.

Just then the imperturbable calm of the café was shattered by a shriek.

"Mama, help me!" A little boy at one of the tables had toppled out of his chair, a big shaggy dog jumped upon him and lapped his face. The dog, a stray, had, in passing, playfully leaped upon the child and thrown him off balance. Even before the mother could reach her son, the waiter was shooing the unwelcome creature away. The little boy, terrified, was flailing his arms in all directions. Quickly his mother collected him in her arms and began to console him.

At the outcry, "Mama, help me!" Pedro's father stopped playing, wheeled around and stared at the scene from a distance. His guitar hung loosely at his side. Not until the child's choked sobs had subsided did he turn around again. Slowly his eyes sought the spot a few yards away where Pedro stood. He gazed at Pedro strangely, stunned. His mouth twisted.

"What are we doing here?" he whispered hoarsely. His eyes darted over the blur of unfamiliar faces before him.

Pedro felt a deep ache for him. His father seemed so small and lonely and lost. Pedro walked over and reached out for his father's arm. As he touched the weathered corduroy jacket he felt a quiver and then a yielding.

His father looked down at him, with brow knitted, his eyes squinted like someone deeply absorbed in figuring out a puzzle. Pedro had the feeling that the two of them were suspended there, all by themselves. The other people didn't matter. . . . And then as if something had suddenly stirred inside him, his father's eyes unveiled.

The tension of the pause broke and Pedro heard his father's voice, singing, singing for the first time since his wife's death.

> *En los brazos te tengo,*
> *y me da espanto,*
> *¿qué será de ti, niño,*
> *si yo te falto?*

> In my arms I hold you,
> and I am afraid,
> what will befall thee, child,
> if I am gone?

It was the lullaby Pedro's mother used to sing to him. The sounds came slow and clear, not soft, the way she had crooned them with her child on her lap, but questioning, despairing.

The *tocador* hung onto the words, as if finding their meaning for the first time. And all the while his eyes remained fixed on Pedro. The words were dedicated to the boy, and they were sung by the father, for himself and for the absent mother. By the time the song was over a peacefulness rested on his face.

The audience, spellbound by the man's intensity, now listened in utter silence. At the end no one clapped. There was a hush.

Moments later, Pedro's father with a gaze open and tender leaned over and kissed his son's forehead.

"*Hijo mio, hijo nuestro*, my son, *our* son," he said quietly.

While listening to his mother's song Pedro felt his heart drumming in his ears, his throat swelling like a balloon about to burst. Now as he looked up at his father, the severe mask all gone, his eyes overflowed. They allowed his tears to come, freely.

The owner from one of the four cafés approached. "You are a magnificent guitarist," he said in halting Spanish. "*Magnífico*. And your boy, he seems so clever."

Pedro's father, still looking at Pedro, acknowledged the compliment with a murmured *gracias*.

"I am looking for a promising young fellow to train to work here in the café, to run errands, to learn everything. I'm told that Spanish boys are good workers. Would you like to apprentice him?" Though there was no answer, the owner, unaware that he was intruding went on unconcernedly, "Meanwhile, you can stroll all through Paris and play your guitar. I tell you, you'll get rich . . . Well, what do you say?"

There was a pause. Pedro's father shook his head, and then a hesitant smile invaded the familiar, now deepened creases of the *tocador*'s face.

"Come, Pedro," he said. "It's time to go home to your mother's house."

Pedro clutched his hand.

It took the *tocador* and his boy two months to make their way back through France and across Spain, singing at cafés, taking all the rides they could get, sleeping in fields of poppies and daisies when it was fair, and at inns when it was not. By now Pedro, sun-tanned and sturdy, could match his steps to his father's long strides.

"Ah, Pedro, you are a man now," his father told him. Pedro smiled; he felt more manly. "I'm proud of you," his father went on, "and Mama would be too."

Pedro linked onto his father's arm. "Next month I'll be twelve."

"Yes," said his father, "and that means we

must buy you a fine goat." Pedro beamed happily. His father had remembered the promise.

At last one day when the sun was lazily embroidering the sky in apricot and tangerine threads, the travelers entered the *pueblo*. By the stream at the edge of town, some women were laundering and one called out: "*Vaya con Dios.*"

And Pedro's father answered in the gentlest voice Pedro had ever heard, "*Vaya con Dios.*"

They walked past the gypsies weaving baskets in front of their cave, and then on to the center of town. There were all the familiar shops, the blacksmith where the horses of the village got their new shoes, and the grocery where everything from rice to candy to flypaper was sold. Everything looked so good after their long absence. At the bakery they bought a freshly-baked hot loaf, and at the market a kilo of fish.

As they climbed the steep, cobblestone street that led to their house, Pedro felt as if he were being tugged by an invisible cord and he began

to run. There it was. The house stood before
him with its familiar lines, its whiteness sur-
rounded by the terra-cotta earth, and enveloped
in the pungent smell of geraniums. The house
looked smaller than he remembered. His heart
leaped with anticipation as his father reached
for the key that for months had hung untouched
on the window ledge. He watched his father
walk to the door and turn the key in the lock.

The door creaked open on its iron hinges and
fingers of light penetrated the darkness. The
house was as chill and damp as the earth in win-
ter, and had a musty, closed-in smell. Pedro
felt a stab of sadness as sharp memories of his
mother rushed forth. Nothing was changed in
the house. Everything occupied the same place.
The shattered vase still lay on the floor where it
had dropped on their last day here. The pieces
would be scooped up—perhaps they could be
glued together.

From the threshold Pedro gazed at the *nafre*
in the corner waiting to be lit, the clock on the

shelf waiting to be wound, the garlands of garlic, onions, and red peppers hung in the kitchen
ready to be used.

Pedro straightened up. This was their place,
and it was waiting for them. Their spirits had
been aired like a pillow fluffed out in the sun.

"Let's go in, Papa," said Pedro, squeezing
his father's hand tightly.

"Open the shutters, my son, and let in the
light."

ABOUT THE AUTHOR

Toby Talbot has written or edited a number of books for children, including *Coplas: Folk Poems in Spanish and English,* published by Four Winds Press. She has translated several books of Spanish literature and philosophy. A former education editor of New York's *El Diario,* Ms. Talbot currently teaches Spanish at Columbia University. She lives in New York City with her husband and three daughters.